W9-BWW-571

For Mum
TR

For Mum
CG

First US edition 2022

Library of Congress Catalog Card Number pending
ISBN 978-1-5362-2035-3

APS 26 25 24 23 22 21
10 9 8 7 6 5 4 3 2 1

Printed in Humen, Dongguan, China

This book was typeset in Chaparral Pro.
The illustrations were done in mixed media.

Candlewick Press
99 Dover Street
Somerville, Massachusetts 02144

www.candlewick.com

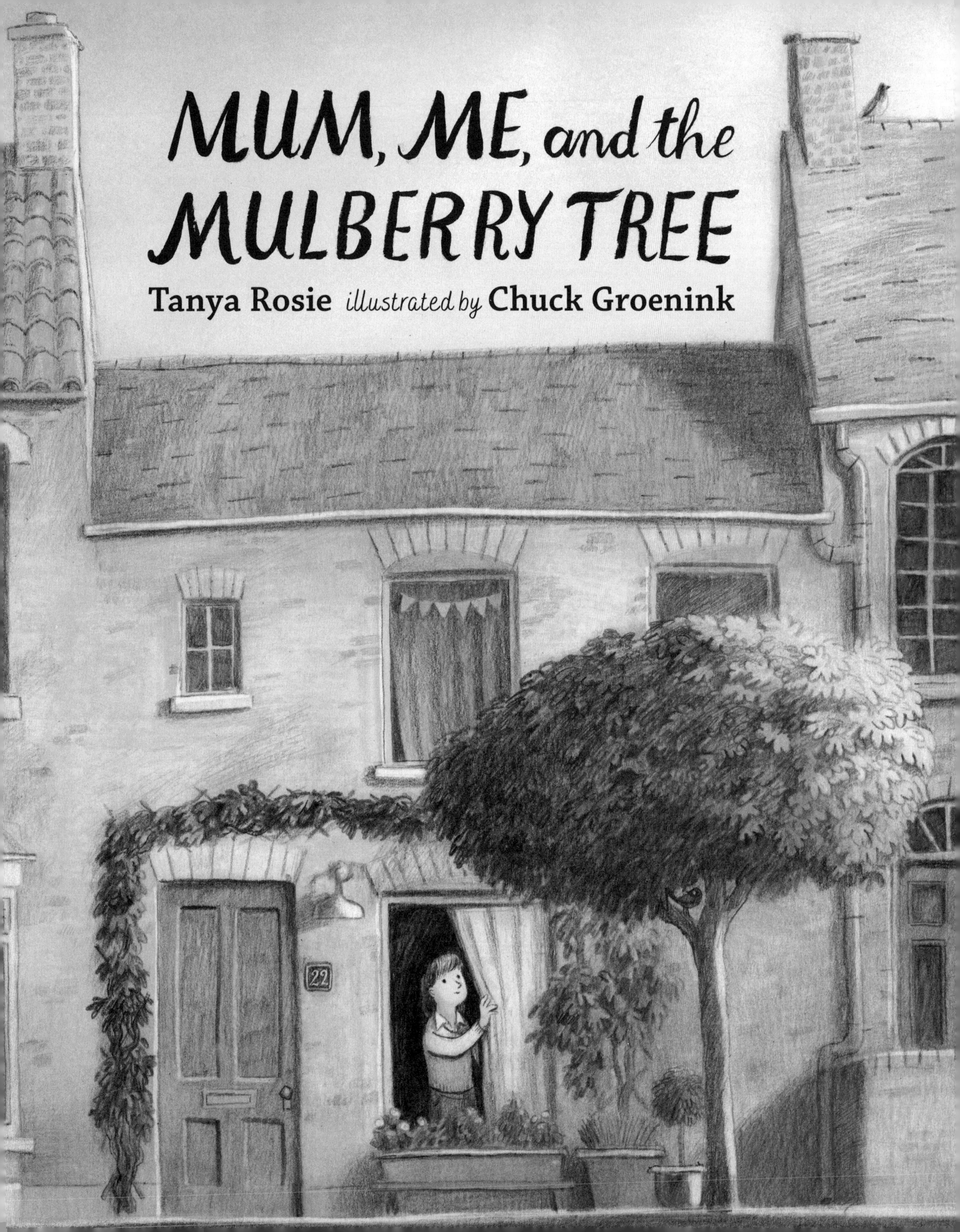
MUM, ME, and the
MULBERRY TREE
Tanya Rosie illustrated by Chuck Groenink
22

AS THE SUN starts to rise,
Mum softly shakes me.
“Time to wake up and
get ready.”

I fasten my buttons and tie my own laces.
Mum holds out a hand, strong and steady.

Now on to the bus! We know the road well.

We sit side by side, knee by knee.

We've brought buckets and tubs—every tub Mum could find!

We're going to visit . . .

our tree.

The grass is so long, it's wild when it waves.

I point to the field with glee.

Mum squeezes my hand; her other hand's full.

We're here! We're here!

Mum and me.

Will there be many, and will they be ripe?
Mum whispers, "Just wait and see."

I see a branch stir, stroked by the breeze.
It feels like “Hello!” from our tree.

And then we're beside it,
and then we're beneath,
under the cool canopy.

Mum lifts me up high,
and I see them all glitter—
the jewels of this mulberry tree.

Now we pick and we pluck. We eat as we go!
Mum saves her most purple for me.
There's juice on our hands and stains down our shirts
as we skip round the trunk, one, two, three.

When we stop for our lunch, we feel a first raindrop.
"Quick," laughs Mum. "Back to the tree!"
We share each treat to the *drip*, *drip* of drizzle,
to the bumbling *buzz* of bee.

Then Mum starts to climb,
up, up, and up,
finding berries the world can't see.
I worry and call, "Mum, don't go *too* high."
But she's safe in the arms of our tree.

When the sun sets, it's like the setting of summer.
My heart sinks like a stone in the sea.
We head back home, my head in Mum's lap,
in the window a last glimpse of tree.

Mum lights up the house and warms up the oven.

We roll out the dough for the pastry.

Together we whip cream into cotton ball clouds.

Then . . . *Ding!* There it is . . .

“The pie is ready!”

We ***mmm*** and we ***hmm***; we savor our slices,

oh, so tangy, so tasty!

My mouth is sticky. Mum wipes it and smiles.

"You're delicious, too, my baby."

AS THE MOON starts to glow,
Mum takes me to bed.

She leans in close and kisses my head.
“Good night,” she sings as I shut each of my eyes.
I see that deep red. I taste that sweet pie.

Outside the window, a bird chirps a last song.
It sounds young and happy and free.
Until this time next year, I know I'll be dreaming . . .

mulberry dreams of Mum and me.